Many Ways to Say
I Love You

Many Ways to Say
I Love You

WISDOM FOR PARENTS AND CHILDREN
FROM MISTER ROGERS

FRED ROGERS

HYPERION

NEW YORK

Library of Congress Cataloging-in-Publication Data has been applied for

ISBN 1-4013-0170-3

Hyperion books are available for special promotions and premiums. For details contact Michael Rentas, Assistant Director, Inventory Operations, Hyperion, 77 West 66th Street, 11th floor, New York, New York 10023, or call 212-456-0133.

FIRST EDITION

10 9 8 7 6 5 4 3 2 1

THIS BOOK IS DEDICATED TO ALL THOSE
WHO HAVE CARINGLY GIVEN US LOVE
AND TO THOSE WHO
GRACIOUSLY RECEIVE OUR LOVE.

CONTENTS

by Joanne Rogers

My own wish for children and parents alike is that they learn to find love and joy even amidst the world's and their own imperfections . . .

—FRED ROGERS

Those of us who are parents certainly know about "imperfections"—our own and our children's! Parenting is a struggle. I was always touched when people would tell me how much they've learned from Fred that's helped them in their parenting, but I have a hunch that they thought he had some magical gift with children. He and I had to work at being good parents . . . just like everyone else.

As I think about our own early experience in parenting, what I remember is that we were a not-so-young mother and father, both thirty-one years old, when our first son was born. We had been married for seven years, and we were overjoyed to be a family at last. I can also remember how insecure Fred and I both felt over the prospect of taking care of this tiny person. At the same time, we felt ready for the challenges ahead. Our second son was born just twenty-one months later. Those were busy but happy times for Fred and me and for both sets of grandparents. It was a great blessing that both boys were essentially very healthy, so we were gently eased into parenthood.

Fred was understandably very protective of our family life, but he did share some of his feelings about our parenting in some writing that he did a number of years ago:

> Looking back over the years of parenting that my wife and I have done with our two boys, I feel good about who we are and what we've done. I don't mean we were perfect parents. Not at all. Our years with our children were marked by plenty of inappropriate responses. Both Joanne and I can recall many times when we wish now we'd said or done something different. But we didn't, and we've learned not to feel too guilty about that. What gives me my good feelings is that we always cared

and always tried to do our best. Our two sons are very different
one from the other; yet, at the core of each of them there seems
to be a basic kindness, a caring, and a willingness to try.

I've heard young parents complain about the way they were treated by their own parents, and they say, "I'll *never* make that mistake with *my* kids!" And probably the most honest response to that is, "Perhaps you won't make *that* mistake, but you'll surely make your own different ones." Well, we certainly made our share of mistakes. But whatever we did, our sons appear to have forgiven us, and now that they're grown, that core of "kindness, caring, and willingness to try" is still very much intact. They know our love for them was always unconditional.

As Fred said in one of his "Neighborhood" songs, "There are *many* ways to say I love you," and of course, we all have our own ways of expressing that love. But however we say it, Fred believed deeply that love is essential in the life of a child. I remember when he first really understood what that meant. Many years ago I traveled with Fred to London where he had the rare privilege of attending a case presentation by Anna Freud, the noted child analyst and daughter of Sigmund Freud. The child whose case was being discussed that day came from the most unhealthy emotional environment imaginable and was having some problems with the staff, yet was functioning rather well in the group. Typically in a case study, what comes next is the expert's perspective of the child's problems. But what Anna Freud said that day was something very different: "We need to try to understand why, in spite of all the trauma, is this child emotionally healthy and thriving?" Fred was fascinated with her question. What helps a child to be able to grow into a confident, competent, caring human being, in spite of being at risk in so many dimensions?

That focus on the positive made such an impression on Fred that it became a central part of his philosophy. I think it resonated so deeply with him because he always felt more comfortable focusing on strengths rather than on weaknesses, maybe in part because of his spiritual background.

Years later, he found his own way to answer Anna Freud's question:

The roots of a child's ability to cope and thrive, regardless of circumstance, lie in that child's having had at least a small, safe place (an apartment, a room, a lap) in which, in the companionship of a loving person, that child could discover that he or she was loveable and capable of loving in return. If a child finds this during the first years of life, he or she can grow up to be a competent, healthy person.

Guided by Dr. Margaret McFarland, his mentor in his graduate work in child development, Fred learned firsthand what it meant to offer that kind of safe place for children and their closest caregivers. Under her supervision, he began working directly, one on one, with young children. That's where he learned about providing an extra measure of security that could help strengthen both children and their parents.

A few years later, when Fred set about to create his children's television program, that approach became the cornerstone for his "Neighborhood." He set out to provide a kind, caring, and safe place—a place that was safe for all children, and for all kinds of feelings. As a "neighbor," he wanted to support what is healthy in children. He sometimes made a point of defining his relationship for children, saying something like, "I'm a television friend. That's different from being a father or a mother. In our family, there are times when our sons and I get angry with each other and have to work things out. Family life is like that."

With his remarkable ability to connect with his viewing audience on a one-to-one basis, he succeeded in giving love through this often all-too-impersonal medium. In his mind, there was sacred space—"hallowed ground"—between what he was giving through the television and what the viewer was receiving.

So many parents told Fred that *Mister Rogers' Neighborhood* was a safe place for them as well. They thanked him for helping them be better able to see the world through the eyes of their children—and for nourishing *them* with the messages of love and humanness that we all need, no matter how old we are. He wanted to be an ally for them, so you can imagine how much it touched him to hear them say, "You've made me a better parent."

Over the years Fred also received thousands of letters from parents who wrote about some concern they had about their children and asked for some advice. What he heard in their comments were their strengths—how much they obviously cared about their children. He knew that's what would help them keep working on dealing with their concerns. Often he closed his response with, "Your children are truly fortunate to be growing up in your caring family." I'll never forget one particular letter that he shared with me from a mother who wrote back, saying that she was moved to tears from those words—and that it strengthened her long afterward.

Somehow Fred was able to find a balance between applauding parents and reminding them of how complicated and challenging parenting is. I think he trusted that if we as parents feel we're being supported, we'll find the best in ourselves to give to our children . . . we'll find the patience to weather the ups and downs of everyday family life . . . we'll find the willingness to look for help if we're struggling.

Fred lived to see our older son become a wonderful father. Sadly, he missed the birth of our younger son's child by a few weeks, but he knew the birth was coming soon and was excited for our younger son to become a parent. I have been fortunate to witness both sons' fatherhood—and to see such healthy traits in all three of our grandsons. I am deeply grateful to my sons and to Fred, whose beautiful spirit gave them life and dwells in them.

What
We Bring
from
Our Past

What a miracle of continuity each new baby brings into this world! A firstborn, particularly, may arouse in his or her parents feelings that are both very new and very old. And as we adjust to parenthood, we bring to the task so much that comes from the way our parents raised us and their parents raised them . . . and so on, back to times and people and places that no one can any longer remember. Becoming a parent does bring new feelings, but in another sense, those feelings are as old as mankind.

Being a giver grows out of the experience of having been a receiver—a receiver who has been lovingly given to.

Since we were children once, the roots for our empathy are already planted within us. We've known what it was like to feel small and powerless, helpless and confused. When we can feel something of what our children might be feeling, it will help us begin to figure out what our children need from us.

It may be a little easier if we know ahead of time that some of the intensity we feel as we try to help our own children with their hard times is very likely related to what we went through ourselves when we were children. Even if our childhoods were relatively problem-free, growing always presents us with difficulties to be overcome . . . and the memories of these difficulties are so easily awakened as our children encounter similar difficulties of their own.

A mother said to me: "I wonder how many parents feel the way I do—trying to juggle the raising of our own children while I'm still sorting out my own childhood problems!"

I tried to reassure her that most parents probably had those same feelings. After thinking about it, though, I realized that she had touched on an important part of what raising children means to *all* of us.

When a person becomes a parent, he or she will not only live through the *experiences* of the new child but will relive many of the experiences of the old child he or she once was. Reliving is an inseparable part of parenting.

How we dealt with our own earliest experiences has a lot to do with how we cope with the ones that come later—and with how we help our children encounter their first challenges. For instance, if we had a fearful and difficult time getting injections at the doctor's office when we were little and really hated it, that is going to affect our ability to help our children through their own experiences with injections and doctors. Children pick up very quickly on how we are feeling at times that are difficult for them—to the point that our feelings become part of their feelings.

Feelings from childhood—both the pleasant and the tough—never go away. They may get hidden, but they're always part of who we are.

I Did Too

Did you ever fall and hurt your hand
    or knee?
Did you ever bite your tongue?
Did you ever find the stinger of a bee
Stuck in your thumb?

Did you ever trip and fall down on
    the stairs?
Did you ever stub your toe?
Did you ever dream of great big
    grizzly bears
Who wouldn't go?

I did too.

It seems the things that you do,

I did too when I was very new.

I had lots of hurts and scares and worries

When I was growing up like you.

Have you noticed how delighted young
children are to hear their parents tell stories
of things they did when they were little?
Part of that delight comes from shared
moments of closeness with a person you
love, and part of it comes from hearing that
someone you love had the same kinds of
feelings you now have, did some of the same
things, got dirty, got in trouble, laughed
and cried and felt afraid. I've heard
children say, "Grandpa got mad at Daddy
just the way Daddy gets mad at me
sometimes."

Stories of our childhoods tell our children something else: They let our children know, without our even having to put it into words, that being little and vulnerable doesn't last forever. Just as we grew from babies to children to who we are, so will they.

The closer we can come to understanding what our children might be feeling, the more empathic toward them we can become. Instead of taking children's misbehavior personally, for instance, we can begin to understand *why* it might be happening. Understanding invariably leads to finding caring ways to help.

While empathy allows us to see things from our child's point of view, we still need to keep our own adult perspective as the parents. Even though we might remember how angry we were as children when an adult told us to stop playing and get ready for bed, we need to balance that empathy with being a limit-setting parent. Children really do want their parents to make rules and set limits—even though they may "test" us. They want—and need—their parents to be in charge.

Love, I feel quite certain, is at the root of all healthy discipline. The desire to be loved is a powerful motivation for children to behave in ways that give their parents pleasure rather than displeasure. It may even be our own long-ago fear of losing our parents' love that now sometimes makes us uneasy about setting and maintaining limits. We're afraid we'll lose the love of our children when we don't let them have their way.

So we parents need to try to find the security within ourselves to accept the fact that we and our children won't always like

one another's actions, that there will be
times when we and our children won't be
able to be "friends," and that there will
be times of anger within the family.

Grandparents are both our past and our future. In some ways, they are what has gone before; in others, they are what we will become.

From the very beginning of our lives, we've had a natural need to receive. Without it, we couldn't have grown. We wouldn't have wanted nourishment; we wouldn't have wanted care. And what we must realize is that we do not outgrow this need to receive. Receiving times are for everybody, and so are giving times.

I remember when my mentor Dr. Margaret McFarland said, "You know, Fred, in everyone's life there are times for looking back at who we've been and what we've done, times for remembering who cheered us when we were sad, who held us when we were mad, who laughed with us when we were happy."

I wonder what you may have in your personal history that has been a comfort to you from the time of your childhood? Reach inside yourself and try to remember what someone you loved said to you or did for you when you needed comfort as a child.

Whatever you discover could be one of the most significant parts of your family's tradition. Whatever has helped you has a very good chance of helping your children, too.

We all long to be cared for, and that
longing lies at the root of our ability to
be care-givers.

Your history is who you are, and there never has been—and never will be, in the history of the earth—another person exactly like you.

Most children love to hear about their parents' childhood: What did you like to play with when you were a child? What did you like to eat? What were some of your family holiday or mealtime traditions? Children also love to hear about their own history—about when they were born or the funny things they said when they were first learning to talk. Knowing about their own personal history can help them appreciate that "then" is very much connected to "now" throughout their life.

I think I've been interested in children because my parents and grandparents—my early teachers—really valued children. For them, children were to be seen *and* heard, and what we said and thought mattered to them.

Parents are like shuttles on a loom. They join the threads of the past with the threads of the future and leave their own bright patterns as they go, providing continuity to succeeding ages.

No husband and wife were ever raised in exactly the same ways by their parents. We all bring echoes from our own childhoods to the task of raising our children when it's our turn.

And, of course, watching and learning as we grow also bring us to different conclusions about how we want to raise our children.

"But isn't it important for mothers and fathers to be consistent with one another in setting rules and dealing with discipline?" people often ask. They're asking an important question.

I believe that consistency is helpful and even necessary for children's healthy emotional growth, but the consistency I mean is *each* parent's separate consistency. Knowing what to expect from a mother or a father day by day is part of the security a young child needs as he or she strives to grow in his or her own way.

But something else children need is the understanding that *every* person is different. With that understanding can come children's appreciation of their own differences and the courage to be who they are—each one different from everybody else.

Our culture places such a high value on friendships and on being "popular." It's understandable that parents want their children to have friends. One of life's greatest joys is the comfortable give-and-take of a good friendship. It's a wonderful feeling not only to have a good friend, but to know how to *be* a good friend. No wonder we adults are concerned when our children have problems making friends!

Maybe you have some fond memories of your childhood friendships, but you might also remember times when you felt like an outsider and longed for friends. Most of us have had a variety of social experiences. If we can remember the different kinds of friendships that we've had through the years, we can better understand that our children probably will have them, too.

Even though, as empathetic parents, we try our best to "remember," we can't understand the world exactly the way we once did as little children, or see the world the way our children are seeing it now.

We have all been children and have had children's feelings, but many of us have forgotten. We've forgotten what it's like not to be able to reach the light switch. We've forgotten a lot of the monsters that seemed to live in our room at night. Nevertheless, those memories are still there, somewhere inside us.

How we deal with the big disappointments in life depends a great deal on how the people who loved us helped us deal with smaller disappointments when we were little.

It may be easier for us if, as children, we were allowed to have our angry feelings and if someone we loved let us know that those feelings were a normal part of loving and being loved. It will certainly have helped us if we learned to talk about those feelings and express them in healthy ways.

Parents are extra-vulnerable to new tremors from old earthquakes. For instance, when we leave our children in child care or in preschool for the first time, it won't be just our child's feelings about being separated from us that we will have to cope with, but our own feelings as well—from our present and our past, from when we were children and struggled with our own feelings of being away from loved ones.

I think of how I've grown—how I've changed—through my years of being a father. How I not only learned to change a diaper, but even learned to listen for the cry which told me the diaper needed changing. I learned about child safety and nutrition and what it was like to feel proud and sad and angry and delighted at my own relationship with my very own child. I even learned to appreciate parents more—my own parents included.

I realized that it wasn't all that easy to be a parent. And all along the way, I've been discovering lots of things about myself—what I was like when I was the various ages of our sons. Their growing has evoked memories of my own growing, and I've had another chance to work out some things I thought I'd finished and forgotten.

Isn't it amazing how much we bring of
who we've been to whatever we do today!
And that happens all through life.

In thinking about family times together, I realize that I have come back to the very best reason parents are so special. It is because we parents are the holders of a priceless gift, a gift we received from countless generations we never knew, a gift that only we now possess and only we can give to our children. That unique gift, of course, is the gift of ourselves. Whatever we can do to give that gift, and to help others receive it, is worth the challenge of all our human endeavors.

Growing as
Parents

Parents don't come full bloom at the birth of their first baby. In fact, parenting is about growing. It's about our own growing as much as our children's growing, and that kind of growing happens little by little.

It's tempting to think "a little" isn't significant and that only "a lot" matters. But most things that are important in life start very small and change very slowly, and they don't come with fanfare and bright lights.

For all parents, the birth of a child
means that life will never be the same
again, and each new child forces changes
and reorderings of old relationships.
Our pleasures and pains are now bound
up in someone else's life, someone else's
needs, experiences, feelings, triumphs,
and misfortunes, and bound more closely
than they ever have been before.

Our children are richer when we let them know that we, even as adults, want to grow, too, and that we hope to keep growing all our lives.

I'm Taking Care of You

I'm taking care of you,
Taking good care of you.
For once I was very little, too,
Now I take care of you.

While some challenges our children face may make us anxious, they also present us with one of the great opportunities of parenting—the chance to resolve these lingering anxieties of our own. That's why I often say that "children offer us another chance to grow." Going through an experience with your child that was once frightening to you when you were a child allows you to find ways to comfort not only your own son or daughter, but also the child that has remained within yourself. You're an adult now and you can use your adult perspective to make a difference in your children's present and your own past.

The relationship a parent has with a first-born is different than with any subsequent children. That difference is natural, but it can sometimes make a parent feel guilty. The birth of a first child is the birth of parenthood for that child's mother and father. As new parents, they suddenly open the door for all kinds of new learning—not only about their baby, but also about parts of themselves they thought were long forgotten.

Being a parent is a complex thing. It involves trying to feel what our children are feeling and trying to know just how much to do to help them with what they cannot yet do for themselves. It involves understanding the difference between sympathy and empathy.

Doing just enough for somebody so that person can grow and do all that he or she is capable of doing—that's a large order.

I received a letter from a parent who wrote: "Mister Rogers, how do you do it? I wish I were like you. I want to be patient and quiet and even-tempered, and always speak respectfully to my children. But that just isn't my personality. I often lose my patience and even scream at my children. I want to change from an impatient person into a patient person, from an angry person into a gentle one."

Just as it takes time for children to understand what real love is, it takes time for parents to understand that being *always* patient, quiet, even-tempered, and respectful isn't necessarily what "good" parents are. In fact, parents help children by expressing a wide range of feelings—including appropriate anger. All children need to see that the adults in their lives can feel anger and not hurt themselves or anyone else when they feel that way.

If you like to make things out of wood,
or sew, or dance, or style people's hair, or
dream up stories and act them out, or play
the trumpet, or jump rope, or *whatever* you
really *love* to do, and you love that in front
of your children, that's going to be a far
more important gift than anything you
could *ever* give them wrapped up in a box
with ribbons. And what's more: The last
thing in the world you have to be is perfect
at it. It's the spirit that gives that kind of
gift its wings.

There's a longing that everyone shares, parents and children alike, and that is the longing to have something to give that is acceptable to others.

When a baby is born, parents often feel that they would like to give that baby a perfect life. It's a very natural feeling, but of course not a very realistic one, especially if "perfection" to those parents means "no trouble, no tears, no fights, constant providing for every need, every minute." Every parent soon discovers that kind of perfection is far from possible (even if it were desirable). Nighttime feedings and diaper changes and stomach pains and growing pains and jealousies and all the rest enter the picture very early and parents are forced to realize, often sadly, that the "perfect," untroubled life is just a fantasy. In daily living, tears and fights and doing things for ourselves, are all part of our ways of developing into an adult.

When our sons were born, I thought, how in the world will I ever be a father to teenagers? Well, thankfully, you don't have to be right away. It's so important to be able to be the father of a one-year-old before you're the father of a two-year-old.

Life is marked by failures and setbacks and slip-ups, as much as by hard-won satisfactions and sudden discoveries of unexpected strength. We need to help children understand that for us, as for them, life is made up of *striving* much more than attaining.

Each of our life journeys is unique. No child will take the same journey as the parent, and no parent can determine what a child's journey will be.

There's mystery in raising children: As your children grow and develop their unique talents, you can't control every aspect of their lives. For example, we can offer children music lessons and do all we can to encourage them to appreciate music; but, if making music isn't their way of expressing themselves, we have to trust that they'll find their own ways.

It may be painful for us to see our children modifying or even rejecting ideas that were important to us and adopting others that could never be comfortable for us. But out of that difference may come the reinforcement of two other important values. One is tolerance, and the other is awareness that people who disagree over the things they hold dear really can live together in love and respect.

It is one of the paradoxes of parenting, and often a painful paradox, that even as our children need us for love and trust, they also need us for honest differing. It may be more than just differing over limits and rules. It may be differing about some of what we represent in the way of culture, traditions, and values.

If we expect our children to always grow smoothly and steadily and happily, then we're going to worry a lot more than if we are comfortable with the fact that human growth is full of slides backward as well as leaps forward, and is sure to include times of withdrawal, opposition, and anger, just as it encompasses tears as well as laughter.

"Letting our children go" is a lifelong process for parents, one that we wrestle with again and again. Each parent has to wrestle with it in his or her own way.

Parents can set the example by just being themselves rather than trying to be perfect parents. As a parent, I found it most helpful to remember the larger picture: that I really did love our sons. But there were times when I couldn't be with them, or when I couldn't give them undivided attention. I've realized that everything does not have to be perfect in order to be effective.

It's a rare parent who hasn't lost his or her temper and reacted verbally or physically. No one is in control all the time. Young children can learn a lot from us when, after the heat of the moment has passed, we can apologize for something we did that was inappropriate. It's good discipline, for us, as well as for our children, to be able to say, "I'm sorry."

What about when parents find themselves
at the end of their ability to cope? I'd help
them know it's understandable that they're
wrestling with thoughts of being "bad
parents" and somehow feel that they're the
cause of the trouble. But I'd like to believe
that mothers and fathers in such dilemmas
could remind one another during the hard
times that, in the persistence of their caring,
they are showing one of the finest qualities
of parents.

No one of us has all the answers. I as a father certainly know that. And there is no one prescription for a child. But listening is so important. Most of us talk a lot and that doesn't leave much time for listening.

The anger we feel toward our children often comes from our own needs. When a child embarrasses us in a store, we feel others are looking at us and thinking, "What a bad parent!" Or maybe after we've spent a lot of time and effort to make a particular mealtime dish, our child refuses to eat it. That can make us feel that it's not only our food that's being rejected, but we ourselves, as well. Sometimes when our children are dependent and whining, we might feel our own impulses to be plaintive and demanding, too. We don't want to be reminded of those feelings in us, and so we

might even surprise ourselves by reacting
really strongly to our children's whining.

When we begin to understand some
of the many feelings we bring to our
parenting, we can be more forgiving of
ourselves. We want to think of ourselves
as nurturing people.

"The amazing thing I've seen in my children," one unemployed father told us, "is that they do grasp the concept of Daddy being out of work. Yet they are so optimistic and encouraging. It helps us go on." That father identifies one of the priceless opportunities of parenthood: the ability to borrow from our children's strength, even as we lend them ours.

We parents are often surprised to find how readily our young children offer *us* comfort at times of honest talk about our feelings. Children need to feel needed just as much as the rest of us do!

Helping has two sides—asking for help and giving help. Whether we're young or old, helping can enrich both the receiver and the giver.

It sure doesn't hurt your children to know
that there are times that you are angry.
When an adult owns up to having certain
feelings, it makes it a lot easier for children
to express their feelings, too.

Society is asking so much of parents and caregivers in today's world: "Make sure your child is safe and healthy"; "Develop routines"; "Set limits"; "Read to your child each night at bedtime"; "Help your child feel secure and loved." And all that is added to other things we're already doing in our lives. Many adults feel that they are falling short in one, if not all, of the "assignments" of their lives. They often feel they are failures.

Well, people are not failures when they're doing the best they can. If parents are managing to cover most of the important bases most of the time, they have every reason to feel good about who they are and what they're doing. Our performance doesn't have to be measured against anyone else's—just against our own abilities to cope.

We've all been bombarded with books on how to raise children. Many of them tell us, "In such and such situation, this is what you say." But no two people in a relationship are the same as any other two people. I don't think that the words are nearly as important as the wanting. I'm very much afraid of formulas. So many of us want shortcuts. What is really important is the basic relationship, and that we must work on all the time.

It can be very hard to trust our own judgments as parents when our feelings seem to be different from those of most other people. The best kind of friends are those who remind us that we are the ones who know the most about ourselves, about our children, and about our relationships with our children.

Watching a child play, either as an interested bystander or by becoming a partner with a child in the play, gives us a wonderful opportunity to learn more about that child—and probably more about ourselves, too.

Maybe you'll also find that, by watching a child at play, you'll tap into some of the playfulness inside you—remembering your own childhood and discovering new things about yourself.

Parenthood is an inner change. We ourselves grow because parenting is so deep and intense.

I think that somewhere deep inside all of us is the powerful longing for a perfect new generation. Maybe since we're not perfect ourselves, we hope to at least create someone who might be.

We all know how meticulously new parents look over their new baby to be sure there are no blemishes—no deviations from what they anticipated. But no matter how beautiful the baby is, there are *always* deviations from what his or her parents anticipated. The greater those deviations, the more those parents need to have the opportunity to mourn—mourn the loss of the image of the perfect child they dreamed they would have. They need to work through the sense of disappointment about things that the child is *not*. They need to give up the image of having the perfect child before they can appreciate the child they really do have.

When my sister was born, I became a brother. I had never been a brother before. Without her, I would never have known what being a brother is really like. When our first child was born, I became a father. I had never been a father before, so he, by his very being, enlarged my identity. When his first child was born, he became a father and I became a grandfather. My grandson's life and his proximity to us allows me to grow in grandparenthood, and by *my* being close to him, I allow him to grow in grandchildhood.

What am I *really* like? I'm a person who has known the pain, the joy, the anger, the sadness, the exhilaration, and the losses of growing up—and all the emotions involved in trying to help my sons grow up. I translate as much of that as I know how to into my work.

The difficult truth is that there are real limits to how much comfort we can bring to loved ones when they hurt. When a baby starts teething, both he and his parents will find themselves up against the limits of comfort: Not even holding or being held will make the pain go away. For a baby, it may be one of his or her earliest lessons that life will have times like that. For the parents, it will be another chance to become more comfortable with what we can and cannot fix.

Almost all of us who have been parents have had the feeling of wanting to give our children perfect lives, lives without pain or sorrow, but of course none of us can. There are many times in life when we can't solve our children's problems or get rid of their fears. Perhaps all we can do is to provide a safe, loving place and a willingness to listen while children work through whatever is bothering them.

Many Ways
of Loving
Each Other

Children who hear that they are loved in many different ways are likely to find their own ways to say it to the people they love— all through their lives.

There Are Many Ways to Say I Love You

There are many ways to say I love you.
There are many ways to say I care about
   you.
Many ways, many ways,
Many ways to say I love you.

There's the singing way to say I love you.
There's the singing something someone
   really likes to hear.
The singing way, the singing way,
The singing way to say I love you.

Cleaning up a room can say I love you.
Hanging up a coat before you're asked to.
Drawing special pictures for the holidays
And making plays.

You'll find many ways to say I love you.
You'll find many ways to understand
    what love is.
Many ways, many ways,
Many ways to say I love you.
Singing, cleaning, drawing, being
    understanding,
Love you.

As a parent, day in and day out, you're a nurturer, comforter, problem-solver, protector, limit-setter, and much more. In the safety of the family, you're helping your child learn how to get along with others, how to deal with rules and limits, how to cooperate, compromise, and negotiate—all qualities that are essential for whatever relationships may be in your child's future.

Every human being needs to be loved and needs to be able to love in return. That is what allows us to be human.

In their very early years, children learn
easily from us parents. They look at us. They
listen to us. They experience the care we
offer them. Just as they take in the
nourishment we give them, they take in our
real qualities, too. Children seem to absorb a
great deal of who their loving caretakers
are. In fact, our children's love for us
parents is the reason they want to please
us—and not displease us. Isn't it amazing to
realize that the real motivation for human
beings behaving toward each other in
pleasing ways begins in—and grows from—
love experienced in infancy?

When we know care is there, life can seem well worth living, even with the ups and downs of our ever-changing world.

The very young baby is ready to receive all kinds of clues as to whether or not he should make the effort to live. And the clues come from the mothering person who takes care of him. The child who is tenderly cared for can, little by little, begin to participate in his own care.

At first, he begins by sucking hard enough so that he'll get enough milk to keep alive. Later, he learns to feed himself and to care for other needs. He takes increasing responsibility for the care of his own body, growing slowly but steadily in the conviction that *he is worth taking care of.*

And little by little that baby grows and takes over more and more of his own care with the support of family, neighbors, television friends, society—he becomes a caring person himself: one who has the capacity of being the available loving adult to the next generation.

At many times throughout their lives, children will feel the world has turned topsy-turvy. It's not the ever-present smile that will help them feel secure. It's knowing that love can hold many feelings, including sadness, and that they can count on the people they love to be with them until the world turns right side up again.

In the disappointment of a defeat, a child
may seem to find little comfort in our
saying, "But you really tried hard, and I'm
proud of you." It takes time to get over a
disappointment. For those children who
have learned to feel valued and loved by
the people they love, these disappointments
do pass.

For a child, moving through life within a family may be a little like being in an airplane: There may be a lot of rough weather outside, and the plane may shake around quite a bit, but inside, you're safe. Sad, scared, and angry, perhaps, but within the special atmosphere of a loving family, even those feelings are safe. When a child learns to trust that there is a loving caregiver right there to help in rough times, he or she can weather most any storm—and ultimately be stronger for the experience.

When there is pain or sorrow in our children's lives, as there is bound to be, there is often no way we can make it go away. Often, our quiet availability is just what children need, far more than they need our coaxings or cajolings or threats or punishments. Our reassuring presence may be enough to help them find inner resources of their own. When children can cope with hard times—drawing on whatever comfort they find from us and from themselves—their parents can be very proud indeed. That ability to cope may be one of the greatest abilities that parents can help their children acquire.

Disciplining a child includes making rules. I prefer to think of this parenting task as "setting limits."

Providing a framework doesn't take away children's individuality. In fact, structure generally helps them to be more free because it provides boundaries. It's like a fence that offers security for what can happen inside the enclosure.

It can be very frightening for a child not to have limits. Not only can the world outside be frightening, but the world inside, the world of feelings, can also be scary when you're not sure you can manage those feelings by yourself.

We feed our children, and as we do so, we help them feed themselves. We keep them clean and warm, and we try to keep them healthy, until they learn to do those things for themselves, too.

In the same way, we provide our children with the limits they need until they learn to exercise *self-discipline*.

Limits need to be set and explained with
care so that children don't come to feel that
we're trying to restrict their capacity to
fall in love with life.

While children certainly need to learn about rules and consequences, they also need the staunch support of grown-ups who help them believe they can make it through.

There's probably no way we can keep our children from feeling sad or angry when they lose, any more than we can keep ourselves from feeling that way. What we can help them understand, though, is that though we appreciate them for what they do, we love them even more for who they are. We can let them know, too, that whether they win or lose, we will always be proud of them for doing the best they can.

Our deep sense of knowing that we are
cared for is probably the most important
thing we human beings have for coping
with the perpetual changes in our bodies,
in our lives, and in the world around us.
We give that sense of being cared for to our
children in the consistency of our care.
As they experience the sometimes unsettling
transitions of day to night, summer to
winter, they come to trust that, even in the
darkness and cold, there will be care until
light and warmth return.

A friend told me about her daughter, Amy, who was angry with her one day. Amy had been sent to her room and, shortly afterward, a note appeared from under her door. It read, "I hate you, Mommy!" When Amy calmed down and came out from her room, she noticed that her mother had put the note on the counter. Turning the paper over, Amy wrote, "I love you, Mommy." Then she added, "P.S. I will never hate you as much as I love you."

That story reconfirms the words of our Neighborhood song, "It's the people you like the most who can make you feel happiest, and maddest." And what a message for us parents—even though we may not appreciate it at that moment—to know that our children's momentary angry feelings won't make their love go away. Children do come to understand that when we set limits and enforce them, we're showing that we love them.

Even people who care deeply about
each other can agree to disagree about
some things.

One of the most essential ways of saying,
"I love you" is by careful listening—listening
with "the ear of the heart."

Anger is a difficult feeling for most people—painful to feel and hard to express. It can help us and our children to remind ourselves that having angry feelings is a part of being human, whether we like it or not. It's just a fact that lovable people get angry sometimes. We can't expect our children never to be angry, any more than we can ask that of ourselves, but we can help them find healthy outlets for the anger that they feel—and help them know the good feeling that comes with self-control.

We all have our limits of patience and endurance, no matter what age we are, and that's something children need to know is natural, human, and acceptable.

It seems to me that to love a child *is* to be outraged with that child at times—to care enough to be really angry. The opposite of love is not hate, it's indifference. I once heard a little boy say to someone, "You can't make me mad. I don't even like you."

It takes thought and emotional energy to work through our own angry moments. If that's what we'd like our children to learn, we're going to have to make it clear to them that we value being able to stop ourselves from doing something that could hurt someone. Children will catch that message from us if we truly believe it's important. And they'll want to make it their own in order to become more like the people they love.

Adults have complex feelings toward children—even as children have complex feelings toward adults. When, for instance, one of our children does something dangerous despite our warnings and rules, we may be angry, frightened, frustrated, and disappointed all at once. It's our love for our children that gives rise to these different feelings, but that's not an easy relationship for young children to understand. In the heat of the moment, it's not easy for us, either, to keep in mind.

At a time like that, our children are most likely to feel our anger, but even as we scold, we need to help them learn where the roots of that anger lie. Trying to be honest with ourselves and our children about what we think and feel helps us continue growing. Encouraging our children to be honest with us about what they think and feel helps them develop their capacity to love themselves and love others.

What children want is for you to talk with them and listen to them. They want your undivided attention. They want you to recognize that their story—the one they bring to your story—is important, too.

We need to try to show our children that we love and value them. By doing so, we can help them learn that there is much in the world to love and value as well . . . and that goes for the people in it, too.

A friend of ours found a way to give her four children the best gift of all. Each week when she does the shopping, she takes only one child. She doesn't buy anything special for that child, but somewhere along the way, she makes sure to say something like, "I really like these times when it's just the two of us together." Young boys and girls don't really want their mothers and fathers all to themselves all of the time, but they do long for the feeling of being best-loved and most beautiful and specially prized *at least some of the time.*

Children aren't the only ones who hunger for individual attention. Friends need time alone together; so do husbands and wives; so do older parents and their grown children.

Here we are, all on this boat together, this floating planet . . . together. I feel blessed even in times of trouble. I wonder how human beings get that feeling? I guess it comes from a long line of people in our life who have, in one way or another, "sung" that song:

It's you I like.
It's not the things you wear.
It's not the way you do your hair,
But it's you I like.

The way you are right now,
The way down deep inside you,
Not the things that hide you,
Not your toys—they're just beside you.

But it's you I like.
Every part of you—
Your skin, your eyes, your feelings,
Whether old or new.
I hope that you'll remember
Even when you're feeling blue,
That it's you I like, it's you yourself,
It's you. It's you I like.

Above all, I think that the willingness and the courage to keep on trying develops best if there is someone we love close by who can lend us some of the strength we do not yet have within ourselves. I don't mean someone who will do a task for us, but rather someone who will share our times of trying just by being around and being supportive, someone who can sustain the belief that we can succeed even when we doubt it ourselves. We all need quiet, caring cheerleaders like that—grown-ups as well as children.

When the gusty winds blow and shake our lives, if we know that there are those people who care about us, we may bend with the wind—but we won't break. You're such a gift to your own children. I hope you have such sensitive care in your own life, too.

Growing
as Children

My own wish for children is that they learn to find joy even amidst the world's and their own imperfections . . . that they grow to have a clear but forgiving interior voice to guide them . . . and that they come to have a reasonable sense of shame without an unreasonable burden of guilt.

There is an inner rhythm which sets the normal beat for human growth. We need to respect that rhythm in ourselves, our friends, and in the children with whom we live and work. Healthy babies grow from one phase to another in a predictable way. Human beings have to learn to crawl before they learn to walk. And when we're ready to crawl, we'll find every chance we can to crawl and crawl and crawl—and we don't want people to stop us from crawling, and we don't want people to hurry us to walk.

As children come to be more aware of themselves and their world, they also become aware of how small they are compared to the people who look after them. It may seem that grown-ups get to do all the big and exciting things and make all the decisions, too. But there are special things about childhood and being a child. It helps children feel good about who they are when we adults value the many things children can do. It's a way for us to let them know that we don't want or expect them to be more grown up than they're ready to be—that we really do like them just the way they are.

As children learn, they begin to sort and classify. Often, they do it by way of opposites—big or little, hard or soft, good or bad, black or white, night or day . . . and, of course, same or different. But not many things are all one way or all another, and certainly people aren't.

We all know people who have grown up to dislike other people who are different—because they are different. I've often noticed that when someone feels that way, that person doesn't feel very good about his or her own differences. I think that's where it all begins for us parents: helping our children feel good about their differences so they can be accepting of, and open to, the differences of others. When we help them learn that, we help them build the foundation of compassion.

What matters most is how children feel about their uniqueness, once they do begin to realize that they are different from everyone else. How each one of us comes to feel about our individual uniqueness has a strong influence on how we feel about everyone's uniqueness. Every time we affirm how special our children are to us for being themselves, we're helping them grow into adults who rejoice in the diversity of the world's people.

None of us is exactly like anyone else, but one thing we have in common is our humanity, our very natural, understandable desire to know that at least somebody, *onebody*, thinks there's something special about us, something worth caring about.

One thing is certain: Children need lots of free, quiet time to get used to all that's developing within them. Have you noticed that unhurried time by yourself or with someone you really trust can be the best setting for your own personal growth? It's no different for children.

Children feel far more comfortable and secure when things happen predictably—with routines, rituals, and traditions. Those traditions, big or small, create anchors of stability, especially in rough seas.

Finding the inner readiness to do new things is such an important part of growth. It's one of those things that can be encouraged and supported, but can't be hurried.

A berry ripens in its own good time . . . and so does a child's readiness. Just as the one needs water and sunlight, the other needs the patient reassurance of loving adults who can trust children to grow according to their own timetables. We need to remember that many, many "normal" children depart from the so-called norm, and that *all* children develop the different parts of their minds and bodies on different schedules. That's part of what makes each child one of a kind—something for which we and they can learn to be grateful.

Children need adults who are convinced of the value of childhood. They need adults who can help them to develop their own healthy controls, who can encourage them to explore their own unique endowments. Children need adults—in every walk of life— who care as much for children as they care for themselves.

Respect the child. Treat him as a person. The best thing a person can feel is to be accepted as he is, not as he will be when he grows up, but as he is now, right this very minute.

You're Growing

Someday you'll be a grown-up, too,
And have some children grow up, too.
Then you can love them in and out,
And tell them stories all about
The times when you were their size,
The times when you found great surprise
In growing up.

You're growing, you're growing,
You're growing in and out.
You're growing, you're growing,
You're growing all about.

Most of us can remember how long the summers used to seem and how long it was from birthday to birthday. When we were five, it seemed we'd never get to be ten, and at ten, it seemed it would be forever until we were twenty. So often it is only by looking back at where they have been that children can see that they are growing at all.

There are outward signs of growth that we can help children notice—clothes that get outgrown, pencil marks on a doorjamb that move up as they get taller. There are lots of things that they learn to do that we can remind them they wouldn't have been able to do a month or a year before—tying a shoe, or riding a tricycle. But while these bring satisfaction to children and parents alike, it's children's *inside* growth we particularly need to help them appreciate.

"Growing on the inside" are the words I use when I talk with children about such things as learning to wait, learning to keep on trying, and being able to talk about their feelings and express those feelings in constructive ways. These signs of growth need at least as much notice and applause as the outward kind, and children need to feel proud of them—even more proud than they may feel when that line on the doorjamb goes up another inch.

Although children's "outsides" may have changed a lot over the years, their inner needs have remained very much the same. Society seems to be pushing children to grow faster, but their developmental tasks have remained constant. No matter what lies ahead, children always need to know that they are loved and capable of loving. Anything that adults can do to help in this discovery will be our greatest gift to the future.

Knowing that dependence is both available and encouraged when it's needed makes it easier for young children to learn to be independent.

I have come to realize how important the limits we set for our children are for the development of their creativity: When we won't let them do exactly what they want to do, they have to search out new alternatives.

Parents are likely to feel proud of their children's new capabilities and accomplishments, but they also may regret the passing of earlier times of greater closeness. Three-year-olds, for example, are apt to waver back and forth between dependence and self-assertion. At one moment they may need to act helpless and curl up on a grown-up's lap, while at the next moment they may angrily brush away helping hands and a loving hug. Parents can feel unsettled as they watch their children's independence and individuality unfold. Transitions are seldom smooth.

Working through disappointment can be a healthy experience for both parents and children. Even if it were possible to give someone everything he or she asked for, we would be depriving that person of many ways of growing. We all need to learn that life is a mixture of what is and is not possible.

If we grow up fearing mistakes, we may become afraid to try new things. Making mistakes is a natural part of being human and a natural part of the way we learn. It's an important lesson, at any time of life, but certainly the earlier the better. We all make mistakes as we grow, and not only is there nothing wrong with that, there's everything right about it.

I want children to know that adults can make mistakes, too. Adults don't have to be perfect to be acceptable. People of every age need to know that.

That chores have to be done before play; that patient persistence is often the only road to mastery; that anger can be expressed through words and nondestructive activities; that promises are intended to be kept; that cleanliness and good eating habits are aspects of self-esteem; that compassion is an attribute to be prized—all these lessons are ones children can learn far more readily through the living example of their parents than they ever can through instruction.

There's a world of difference between insisting on someone's doing something and establishing an atmosphere in which that person can grow into wanting to do it.

Being kind means responding to the needs of others—and people can be kind, no matter how old or how young they are.

Children do not develop in a healthy way unless they have the feeling that they are needed—that they enhance the life of someone else, that they have value apart from anything that they own or any skill that they learn.

Children have very deep feelings, just the way parents do. Just the way everybody does. I feel that our striving to understand those feelings, and to better respond to them, is an important task in our world.

Children can carry feelings for a very long time if they don't have an opportunity to talk with someone about them. And when they are able to trust and share their feelings, they often feel free to be more communicative in a variety of ways.

I remember how helpful it was for a teacher
in one of my new schools to say to me,
"Was it hard to leave the old school, and the
teacher and your friends who were there?"
Just her asking me let me know that
somebody understood!

I think that just airing questions helps
children to feel that they're not alone with
their curiosity, their fears, their jealousies,
their angers. . .they're not alone with their
feelings.

I once asked a ten-year-old how he felt about his older brother going off to camp. There were only two boys in that family, and they were competitive and fought a good deal. My young friend said, "It feels great not to have him around . . . but I kind of miss him." I told him I understood how he could feel both ways at the same time. "In fact," I said, "so many people feel two ways about the same thing that our language even has a word for that." I printed the word *ambivalence* on a slip of paper and gave it to him. "That word is *ambivalence*," I told him. "People often feel ambivalent."

His parents told me later that he carried that slip of paper in his pocket for a couple of weeks and that when they'd ask him how he felt about something, his stock answer for a while was, "Oh, ambivalent, I guess." Just knowing that people could feel like that—and that there was even a name for it—seemed to bring him some relief in his struggles with his conflicting feelings.

It can be a big help for any of us to know that our feelings are OK—that there's nothing wrong with having them, and that lots of other people have the same kinds of feelings as well. We'll always have some feelings we're not proud of, and we can certainly be the objects of our own ambivalence.

If we look at our relationships with any of the many, many people in our lives, I believe we'll always find a measure of ambivalence about our parents, brothers and sisters, other relatives, friends, and even ourselves. An ability to accept our ambivalence toward others may be an important ingredient in relationships that are healthy and lasting.

What a gift we all give to children when we encourage them to talk about what makes them happy, jealous, angry, shy, afraid, or proud. Whether we're children or adults, adding to our emotional vocabulary can often add to our ability to cope with what we're feeling. Using words to describe what's inside helps remind us that what we're experiencing is human . . . and mentioning our feelings to others can make those feelings more manageable.

Children's curiosity needs to be encouraged and supported. More important than what we say is letting our children know that we welcome their asking us about anything they don't understand.

No matter what the situation, if we can help children talk about their concerns and their feelings, and really listen to what they tell us, we are letting them know we care deeply about them.

Have you ever watched a frightened child turn to an adult for comfort? Did you notice that the child, in that situation, isn't looking for a diversion? He doesn't want a new toy or a game; what he wants is a relationship. He usually needs reassurance from his parents. He doesn't need or want pat phrases or fancy jargon to help him during stressful times. We should try to understand what he's feeling, and then use our own words or actions to communicate our care and concern.

Over the years, I've come to learn that many of us who have devoted our lives to serving children and their families just hate for the children to be angry—with us or with anybody else! Somehow, we think we've failed if children get angry. We want everybody to be happy.

Well, realistically, nobody's happy all the time, and when children express their anger, they need to trust—way down deep—that we adults will help them find some socially acceptable way of expressing that feeling, some way that's not going to hurt anybody, some way that might help everybody to grow.

Children have very strong feelings. Children love intensely, and they get angry just as intensely. They can be so happy that they laugh out loud, and they can be so sad that they feel their hearts are breaking. And often the way children look at others depends a lot on how they feel within themselves.

When children feel very sad or lonely, they may think life is going to be sad forever. Young children haven't lived through enough of life's ups and downs to know that even if you feel deeply sad now, you will be able to feel joy again at another time—that "the very same people who are sad sometimes are the very same people who are glad sometimes." Children don't learn that simply because we tell them, but it's important for us to let them know that's the way life is. Someone can be very sad for a while, but that while doesn't last forever.

Childhood isn't just something we "get through." It's a big journey, and it's one we've all taken. Most likely, though, we've forgotten how much we had to learn along the way about ourselves and others.

How I wish that all the children in this world could have at least one person who could embrace them and encourage them. I wish that all children could have somebody who would let them know that the outsides of people are insignificant compared with their insides: to show them that *no matter what,* they'll always have somebody who believes in them.

I have tried to encourage children to love and care for themselves and to love the parents who care for them.

That's the way true neighborliness grows—loving others as we first loved ourselves.

ACKNOWLEDGMENTS

At the heart of Fred Rogers' lifework was the circle of giving and receiving: *As we are lovingly given to, we are better able to give to others.* Millions of his viewers have seen and heard it every day through *Mister Rogers' Neighborhood.* Anyone who ever heard him speak remembers his signature minute of silence, during which he encouraged the audience to think about those who helped us become who we are . . . who wanted what was best for us in life . . . who loved us into being.

In the same genuinely loving way, he nurtured each one of us on his small staff at Family Communications, Inc. (FCI), enabling us to carry on his legacy of nurturing others. He was incredibly appreciative of the little things we'd offer him—a kind note, a homemade treat, or a story about a child. He elevated those moments and cherished them, just the way he did in his song "Many Ways to Say I Love You": "Cleaning up a room, picking up your coat before you're asked to do it, cooking something someone really likes to eat, making something special for the holidays, and making plays." In his eyes, those were acts of love . . . and he elevated them in our eyes as well. Because he was always thanking us for our little acts of kindness, we wanted to do more, and we wanted to be people who appreciate the kindness of others. As he once said, "One kind word has a wonderful way of turning into many."

Through this book, we have an opportunity to acknowledge our own parents, as Fred would say, ". . . whether they're here or in Heaven," to thank them for being there for us and for finding so many ways to let us know we are loved. Without that inner core of love, we would not have been able to survive and thrive—and be able to do this work that's so connected to nurturing others. We've come to understand the circle of giving and receiving of love from our parents to us and from us to the children in our lives—a flow of love that has sustained us and helped us grow and learn.

We're again grateful to Bob Miller, president of Hyperion and longtime friend of Fred and FCI, who has helped us keep Fred Rogers' wisdom in the public eye through this series of books. Special thanks to our editor, Mary Ellen O'Neill, who helped us grow through her insight, support, and leadership over the years we've worked together. Thanks, too, to editorial assistant Miriam Wenger, who worked with the manuscript from the beginning, caring for it all along the way, and helping us see it through its final stages.

We're especially grateful to Joanne Rogers, now Chair of the Board of Family Communications, whose warm and lovable nature is at the heart of her parenting and grandparenting, as well as at the heart of her relationship with all our staff. Just as Fred did, she has always recognized the importance of our families in our lives and continues to share herself generously with us.

Here at FCI, we're fortunate to have the leadership of our president, Bill Isler, who guides our work. Working together once again, Hedda Bluestone Sharapan and Cathy Cohen Droz organized the search for quotes, read and reread pages of possibilities, and created an organized structure to the book. Our intern Heather Staunton gave us a great start on this project by carefully and patiently culling quotes from hundreds of pages of Fred Rogers' speeches and articles.

Everyone at Family Communications has had a part in this book. In many ways, we're all doing some aspect of parenting in our work, nurturing families and professionals through our workshops, Web sites, and projects, as we nurture each other as well. We're proud and privileged to carry on Fred's legacy . . . continuing the circle of receiving and giving.

BIOGRAPHY OF
FRED ROGERS

Fred McFeely Rogers was best known as "Mister Rogers," creator, host, writer, composer, and puppeteer for *Mister Rogers' Neighborhood,* which continues to be broadcast on PBS and is its longest-running program.

His journey to the *Neighborhood* began in 1951 during his senior year at Rollins College, when he became intrigued by the educational potential of television. After graduating with a degree in music composition from Rollins, he joined NBC in New York as an assistant producer for *The Kate Smith Hour, The Voice of Firestone,* and the *NBC Opera Theatre.* In 1952, he married Joanne Byrd, a pianist and fellow Rollins graduate.

Returning to his hometown area of western Pennsylvania in 1953, he helped found Pittsburgh's public television station, WQED, and co-produced an hour-long live daily children's program, *The Children's Corner,* for which he also worked behind the scenes as puppeteer and musician. To broaden his understanding of children, Fred Rogers began his lifelong study of children and families at the Graduate School of Child Development in the University of Pittsburgh School of Medicine. There he had the opportunity to work closely with young children under the supervision of Dr. Margaret B. McFarland, a clinical psychologist. He also completed a Master of Divinity degree at the Pittsburgh Theological Seminary and was ordained as a Presbyterian minister in 1963 with the unique charge of serving children and families through the media.

Fred Rogers has been the recipient of virtually every major award in television and education. He has received honorary degrees from more than forty colleges and universities, and in 2002 was awarded the Presidential Medal of Freedom, the nation's highest civilian honor.

In 1971, Fred Rogers founded Family Communications, Inc. (FCI), a non-profit company for the production of *Mister Rogers' Neighborhood* and other materials. Building on its beginnings in broadcast television production, FCI has expanded into almost all forms of media—print, audio, video, training workshops, the Internet, DVD, and traveling exhibits. For information about Family Communications, visit the website (www.fci.org).

The company's ongoing work continues to be guided by Fred Rogers' mission of communicating with young children and their families in clear, honest, nurturing, and supportive ways.